BEING CORDIAL

DESERT ROSE HOOKUPS

MEKA JAMES

CONTENTS

Acknowledgments   v

Chapter 1   1
Chapter 2   6
Chapter 3   10
Chapter 4   15
Chapter 5   19
Chapter 6   25
Chapter 7   29
Chapter 8   34
Chapter 9   40
Chapter 10   47
Chapter 11   53
Chapter 12   59
Chapter 13   65
Epilogue   71

Thank you   77
About the Author   79
Other books by Meka   81
Connect with me!   83

❀ Created with Vellum

ACKNOWLEDGMENTS

To my RChat ladies...I wouldn't know what I'd do without you all. Your constant cheerleading and virtual shoulders to cry on help me more than you know. Special shout out to Lily, Cora and Deana who listened to me whine my way through completion of this book.

To my nephew Josh for answering all my random ass text messages without a second thought. Love you.

To the readers, without you I have no reason to keep sharing my words. Thank you for your support and hope you enjoy this story as much as I enjoyed writing it.

BEING CORDIAL

1

LANA

THE PICTURES ON THE WALL THUMPED WITH THE BASS COMING from next door. It was a Wednesday night for goodness sake. Who the hell threw a party in the middle of the week? The annoying man I lived next to, that's who. I released a frustrated groan and pulled my glasses from my face, dropping them onto the stack of papers beside me.

The disturbance caused Yoda, my three-year-old Chihuahua, to look up at me before he stood, stretched, walked to the other end of the couch, turned three times, and resumed his nap. His back faced me as the ultimate snub.

I'd read the same line of numbers multiple times. The noise from next door was proving to be as frustrating as the person behind it. He who swooped in and snatched up the unit I'd wanted before I'd had a chance to finish weighing the pros and cons of each place.

Spreadsheets—seeing the numbers—that was what I did. But nope, guess some were more impulsive than others. Like Mr. Thoughtless next door.

Of the four complexes I'd narrowed it down to, this one had everything I wanted. A smaller community, lower HOA fees, but a decent amount of amenities with the pool, workout room, and a clubhouse that could host movie nights. I'd picked out exactly which place I'd wanted at each location. Here, it was the end unit on the back half of the subdivision so there was less drive-through traffic. Three bedrooms, a larger living room, and a kitchen with a small sunroom attached to the patio. Not to mention, I got to look out on a distant mountain view and natural desert landscape, instead of my neighbor's backyard like some of the buildings in the center of Desert Rose Station. That was just bad planning.

That unit had been the last end availability in phase three, the final phase which meant I didn't have to deal with long term construction noise and dirt. It was perfect. And two months later, I remained irked over having lost the one I'd scouted out and being forced into making an impulse decision. A decision I'd regretted since moving in.

Thump. Thump. Thump. Thump. My pictures bounced and the pulse in my temple pounded in the same rhythm. I ran my hands through my hair, scrunching it in my fist before letting the curls tumble free. I didn't like confrontation, it wasn't my thing, but how was a woman supposed to think?

I stormed down the hallway, passed my front office that rarely got used, and out my door. My mistake of not stopping for shoes became painfully evident as I had to gingerly walk over the pebbled divider separating my driveway from his. With a frustrated sigh, I shook the nerves from my body before jabbing the doorbell, then hitting it twice more.

As I lifted my finger to hit the button again the door opened with a whoosh. The mid-laugh stopped and the smile dropped from his face the moment he set eyes on me. Two months of living next to him and this was the closest we'd actually come to each other. The fact that I had to look up at him bristled under my skin. At five-nine, I stood eye to eye with most men— taller when I wore heels—and I enjoyed being on even playing ground so to speak. Which meant he had to be at least six feet and another reason his mere presence was a thorn in my side.

"What can I do for you, Ms. Passive Aggressive?" He leaned his lanky body—clad in a plain black T-shirt and gray athletic shorts—against the doorframe and crossed his arms in front of his chest.

I frowned at his greeting. Miss *what* now? Oh, shit. The note I'd left on the windshield of whatever car was parked too close to my driveway and nearly had me blocked in. Leaving a written message was easier. Like memos at work, they were clear, concise, and got the point across without the worry of something being spoken incorrectly.

I crossed my arms and pursed my lips. "Well, you can turn down the music, Mr. Party-In-The-Middle-of-The- Week."

What could only be described as a sarcastic chuckle passed his lips. "So, that's why I've been graced with you talking to me finally? You came to bitch about my music? Surprised you didn't leave a note taped to my door." He scratched at his hair and my eyes were drawn up to the mess of black curls haphazardly sitting atop his head in what I would say was a messy bun that rivaled my own.

His thick, dark eyebrows drew together when his brow crinkled into a deep V. There wasn't a hint of amusement in his rich mahogany eyes. Eyes surrounded by midnight lashes so long they should be criminal on a man. And flawless skin that was a natural warm hue which my damn near pale ass envied. He had the complexion I'd wished my parents would have given me. Instead, Dad's genes won the great DNA battle, at least where my skin tone was concerned. Being this close to him for the first time, damn he was disarmingly good looking. His deep voice which held a New York accent cut through my momentary daze.

"Maybe I should start leaving you notes every time Ren decides to leave unwelcomed gifts out by my patio."

It was my turn to frown. "Who the hell is Ren, and what do they have to do with me?"

He cocked his head to the side and a half-smile tugged at the corner of his lips. Full, dusty rose-toned lips that begged for attention as they stood out from the surrounding close-cut, dark beard.

"Ren. From Ren and Stimpy." He bugged his eyes and his brows rose as if those names were supposed to mean anything to me.

A groan deep from the back of his throat rumbled free. "Your dog. The little rat looking, yappy thing that seems to think my patio is his personal hangout."

I clenched my teeth. Yoda was my baby, and sure he barked sometimes, but he wasn't "yappy" and he sure as hell didn't look like a rat.

I huffed and planted my hands on my hips. "His name is Yoda. And yes, maybe you should have left a note, or knocked on my door if it was an issue."

He shook his head and gave another sarcastic chuckle. "Yeah, right. Me come knock on your door because you've been oh so approachable. We've been neighbors for months, and this is the first conversation we've had. So, knockin' at your door, that ain't likely to happen, Ma. I just clean it up and keep it moving."

His attitude prickled under my skin. I was a friendly person. Mostly.

I started to defend against my note-leaving habits when the grin that had dropped reappeared. A nice smile. Dazzling white teeth that stood out against the dark hairs of his beard. A smile that should not have an effect on me, yet here I stood with strange damn near swoony thoughts unwantedly rolling through my head.

"Don't worry, Ma. I'll turn it down."

I started to respond when another rumbling voice carried toward us.

"Yo, E. What the fuck you doing, jacking off?"

He turned and called back over his shoulder. "Not likely, Ice Queen felt I was worthy enough to have her complain about the music in person."

Ice Queen? *Ice Queen?* I could feel the heat rising up my throat as my blood pressure skyrocketed. And to think I'd been about to thank him for being reasonable.

"For reals?" The speaker stepped into sight and gawked at me like I was some sort of oddity. The look of him with a smug grin on his face made me want to scream.

"In the flesh."

"Just turn it down." I moved to stomp off and immediately regretted it. A pebble lodged into my foot and my storm became a hobble with the sound of their laughter playing as a soundtrack behind me.

2

EMILIO

I PUSHED AGAINST THE KNUCKLES ON MY RIGHT HAND UNTIL I heard two pops and then repeated the process on the left before shaking both out. I'd told Ms. Johnson last time she'd brought me her son's laptop she'd needed to invest in a real virus protector, not the basic free thing that came with the machine. But had she listened? That would be a hard nope, and that was why it sat with me now, and why she was about to be out more than the cost of said virus protection.

Movement outside caught my eye. I turned and groaned. Ren, sniffing around once again on my side of the fence. Ma's ass wanted to get pissed over some music or parking but she let that little beast shit all over the place.

I chuckled quietly thinking about our interaction the other night. No idea what crawled up her ass, but she'd been nothing short of pissy since she'd moved in. In the beginning, I'd attempted to be neighborly. I'd wave or try to be cordial toward her when we happened to be out at the same time, but she was not having it.

Then the notes. A millimeter over the line and she was ranting about being inconsiderate and blocking her in. Shit, if she couldn't back out, that had more to do with her driving than my client's car. I leaned back in my chair waiting to see if she'd come to collect the tiny terror. But she didn't. He sniffed around my grill before he hopped his tiny ass up onto my lawn chair, turned a few times, and started sunning himself like he was king.

I stood to go shoo him away when she stepped into view.

"Yoda, come here." She scooped him up and met my gaze through the glass.

Her light brown eyes were wide as if she was momentarily shocked or embarrassed to see me. I had to admit, when she wasn't scowling at me, she was cute. Her mass of brown curls was tamed today, unlike last night. She had them pulled back in a high ponytail with a few loose strands framing either side of her face.

Seeing her up close had revealed a sprinkle of freckles across her nose. The lack of a scowl didn't last long as the frown that seemed reserved just for me took up place and she whipped around and disappeared around the separator fence.

I shook it off and went back to the task at hand. Music playing, I started digging into the system to clean up the shit-storm that was the infestation of malware. I needed to tell that kid about safer sites if he was going to keep trying to locate free porn online. I threw out that idea. No contributing to the delinquency of a minor. Instead, I'd just install the fucking high-grade virus protection.

My concentration was interrupted by two quick rings of my doorbell. I pushed back from my table and did a stretch as I walked down the hall. Two days in a row I came face to face with the shorty from next door.

"What now? The music ain't even that loud." I crossed my arms and leaned against the doorframe.

She held the tiny animal in her arms, squared her shoulders, and looked up at me. "I just wanted to...apologize for Yoda invading your space." She spoke the words as if it almost pained her to get them out. Damn, she had one hell of a talent of making everything she said sound like an insult.

"Since you're not a dog person and all. Which says a lot about your character. Not liking pets." She pursed her lips and damn near seemed to turn her nose up. Well, if she could, but considering she had to look up at me, that made it a little hard to attempt a "look down."

And there was the actual insult. I cocked my head. "I like pets just fine. I don't like irresponsible pet owners."

She took in a sharp breath and her eyes were mere slits. I pressed my lips together to keep from smiling. Like when she got annoyed last night, a deep red flush started crawling up her neck from behind the stark white button-down she wore. Probably starched knowing how uptight she appeared. I let my gaze travel the length of her body. Gray slacks clung to curvy hips and she wore the ugliest shoes I'd ever seen. Black and bulky with a thick sole and a wide strap that went across the top of her foot. Neither my Gran nor Abuela would put those things on.

The animal yapped and squirmed in her arms. He wasn't that bad looking, cute in his own way, and she had him dressed in a shirt sporting his namesake. She shushed him before leveling her attention back at me.

"I am not irresponsible."

"If you say so. But if you're finished with your crap-ass apology with a side dose of put down I have work to do."

"Work?" She eyed me up and down no doubt making assumptions based on my athletic shorts and ASU T-shirt.

"Yeah, work. You know the nine-to-five people do to pay the bills and shit. Or is that a concept Princess Petty is unfamiliar with?"

She shifted the dog in her arms and thinned her lips. "I know what work is. I come home from my *job* to let Yoda out during my lunch break. Some of us I guess are simply more professional than others."

"Mayhaps or some of us work for ourselves and can wear whatever the fuck we want since we work from home."

That red flush deepened and made its way up to stain her cheeks. No clue why she kept coming over here to embarrass herself, but my patience for this snooty woman was wearing thin.

"Anything else?"

"No." She clipped out the answer then turned to walk back to her unit.

At least the sight of her leaving gave me a nice view. She had an ass on her. I closed the door and headed back to my task. I knew I could be a pain at times, but shit, I hadn't even done anything to her, and yet she was full of nothing but annoyed contempt directed at me.

Giving her hell only made it worse, but she brought it on herself. Someone clearly needed to clue her in on the flies with honey thing because she was a large glass of vinegar with a lemon chaser.

A smile tugged at my lips as I changed tracks to one with extra bass and cranked up the volume on my stereo.

3

LANA

I'D SPENT THREE DAYS TRYING TO IGNORE THE JERK NEXT DOOR. I'd gritted my teeth and refused to take the bait when he'd played his crap-ass music so damned loud. I knew he was doing it on purpose. He had to be, just like he'd turned the volume up after our last conversation. But there he was. Playing basketball across the street with the guy that lived there. Couldn't they work out at the fitness center like normal people instead of using the portable and probably illegal rig?

I paid dues to have those amenities and because of that, there was a certain standard of appearance I expected my neighborhood to have. Cars lining the street and people using their driveways as a gym were not it. Maybe I should complain to the board. I shook my head, dismissing the thought as quickly as it came. Even I wouldn't be that much of a bitch. Besides, it normally was the guy's kids that used it and they always put it away after they were done. There was only one reason why it bugged me more today.

I tried to keep my eyes straight ahead as I drove past them. My annoying neighbor was annoyingly shirtless. He may have appeared to be lanky, but damn it all to hell he was toned. I pulled into my drive and observed the two of them in the rearview while I waited for my garage door to open. Mr. Annoying did some spin move around the other guy and went up for his shot, but it was blocked and knocked down the drive and bounced right into mine.

I parked and glanced back up to the mirror in time to see him drop his head, exchange words with the guy before trotting over to get the offending piece of equipment. He took a deep breath as I stepped out of my car. The action of him squeezing the ball between his hands made the muscles in his sweat coated arms and chest ripple. An intricate tattoo covered his left pec, moved across his shoulder, and stopped mid-way on his upper arm. An uncharacteristic urge to trace the lines tingled in my fingers.

He wasn't body-builder cut with abs on top of abs. He was...sleek. Deceptively muscular with the hidden gems making themselves known in the most mundane of movements. And sweet lord, I needed to keep my eyes up and not even think about letting my gaze drop to the dark blue shorts that hung low on his hips. Or acknowledge the distinct imprint of some other deceptive part of his body that had been eye level when I climbed out of my car. Good gravy it was hot. My entire body warmed from the inside out with most of the heat pooling between my legs.

Numbers. *Think of my numbers and not that, or him, in any sort of way.* He was the loud music-playing, dog-hating jerk from next door. Not someone I should be cataloging images of as fuel for lonely nights with my vibrator. He bounced the ball once before tucking it against his side. "Go ahead and say it."

I frowned. "Say what?"

"Whatever bitchy complaint I'm sure you have."

Thank heavens for him letting the jerk free.

I walked to the trunk of my car to retrieve my bags. *Bitchy...bitchy...*no I would not let him get to me this time. After our last interaction, my neck and face were like a traffic light, which pissed me off. I would not give him the satisfaction of knowing how much he flustered me.

"Why would you think I had any complaint, let alone a 'bitchy' one? You're getting your ball to go back to your childish game."

I grabbed my groceries, closed the lid, and turned to face him. A half-smile pulled at the corner of his lips. He ran his tongue across them and let out an airy laugh.

"Right." He drew out the word which only served to annoy me more.

With a shake of his head, he walked off, bouncing the ball as he went. I would not acknowledge how nice those shorts looked clinging to his behind. Or the way his muscles moved in liquid motion as he dribbled his way back across the street. Adjusting the bags in my arms, I stood frozen, tracking his journey. He tossed the ball to the other guy. They exchanged a few words and when they both looked over at me I hurriedly turned and headed into the house.

Yoda jumped at my ankles when I entered. After setting the bags on the counter, I pulled a treat from the jar, picked him up, and fed it to him. "I do not find him attractive." Yoda shifted, dropping back into cradle position so I could rub his belly. "He doesn't appreciate your sophisticated and totally adorable appearance." I brought him to my face and nuzzled him before placing him back onto the floor.

The comment about Yoda being yappy and rat looking prickled under my skin. Any man that talked about my baby that way—no matter how good he looked shirtless—was not worth my time. I could easily live next door to him and ignore him. I'd done well in the months prior until that blasted music made me crack. I'd simply have to double down on my efforts.

I smiled at the thought as I started to put away my groceries. Hell, I couldn't even remember the last time I saw the neighbor on the other side of me. I think she was an EMT or something based on the uniform. I'd thrown up an occasional wave when she appeared to be coming home as I was heading to work. The roommate I saw maybe a glimpse or two of when she would be outside with her dog. It wasn't like I went out of my way to not interact with them, but life, schedules, things happened. Actively avoiding my annoying neighbor should be just as easy.

Yoda's scratching at the glass got my attention. I headed over, pulled back my sheer curtains and the utilitarian vertical blinds, then cracked the sliding door open enough for him to run out. I made a mental note to check into getting some sort of tie-out contraption for him as to not disturb He-Who-Hates-Animals any longer. "Irresponsible pet owner," I muttered to myself. The nerve of him. Yoda weighed five pounds, how much trouble could he really cause?

I glanced out the door to watch him sniff back and forth along the perimeter of my patio before I picked up my work laptop. Numbers. Facts. Accounting, dealing with invoices and payroll, that's what I needed. Spreadsheets and organization were my Zen and I could focus on that instead of giving my mental energy to the sexy...no shit, not sexy. Not attractive. Damn him and his shirtless-ness and lack of compression shorts to keep certain things hidden and under control. The warmth I'd wanted to attribute to the heat outside once again spread through me and tried to settle between my legs.

I shook my head and hands to get the wonky thoughts and feelings out then lifted the lid of my computer. I blinked once, then twice as I stared at the blank blue screen. The white letters mocked me: Reset to factory default with a blinking Y and N. "No. No. No. No."

I pressed the escape button repeatedly. This was not happening. Not the blue screen of death. It was fine yesterday. Everything was fine yesterday and now restore? Bet it was that stupid fucking update I couldn't bypass. I pressed the power button to do a hard shut down. As I waited for it to reboot, I sent silent prayers to the computer gods that it would work. No such luck.

"Shit. Shit. And triple shit!"

4

EMILIO

"FUCK, FUCKITY, FUCK!"

I glanced over at the barrier between me and Ms. Potty Mouth then went back to flipping my burgers. Ren, however, seemed to have no concerns over his owner's outburst. The tiny beast was too busy sniffing the air and looking at me like I was supposed to share.

More curses filtered out as I plated my burgers and turned off the gas on my grill. "Don't get involved. Don't get involved," I mumbled to myself.

After a long drawn out "shit," I sighed and headed into the house to set down the plate. "What the fuck, Ren, you don't live here." He'd trotted his tiny ass in behind me like he owned the place, ignoring the fact I tried to gently shoo him back outside with my foot. She seriously needed to leash him.

With the runaway animal in hand, I took a deep breath before walking back outside and around the divider fence. Her glass door was opened slightly, presumably so her wayward pet could come and go as he pleased. She paced her living room, phone to her ear. Her face was red and blotchy. The patchy coloring spread down her neck and across her chest. Whatever it was had majorly annoyed her. I chuckled quietly; at least it wasn't me this time.

I probably shouldn't have been checking her out, but maddening or not, she still garnered a second look or two. She'd changed since our encounter in her garage. Ma was a voluptuous woman, I couldn't deny her that. Wide hips, and thick legs and curves for days. The shorts she wore accentuated all her best *assets*. Yeah, if she didn't give off a strong f-off vibe, I'd be down for the hook-up. Though, not sure if getting caught up with the female that lived right next door was a wise move. Especially with one who acted like she could barely stand the sight of me. But if the opportunity ever presented itself...

I put Ren down and he scurried inside. Ma turned and her eyes widened when she saw me standing outside her door. She rolled her eyes, I threw up a hand ready to walk off when she headed toward me, putting her finger up indicating I should wait. For what, I had no damn idea, but wait I did. From the way she moved, I could tell she didn't wear a bra beneath her purple T-shirt that had "I," a red heart, and the Pi symbol underneath it.

Another "fuck" before she ended her call and launched the device across the room onto her couch. A wave of cool air hit me when she opened the sliding glass wider.

"Look, sorry he was on your side again. I was watching him until my computer decided to implode." She pinched the bridge of her nose and puffed out her cheeks on an exaggerated exhale. She glanced back up at me. "Did he..."

"Nah, it's all good, Ma. Ren wanted a burger but I'm not sharing, so I brought him home."

I knew calling the dog by the wrong name would get a reaction and I probably shouldn't have pushed her buttons seeing as how she was already annoyed, but really, it was too easy.

"Look, I'm really not in the mood for your crappy jokes about my dog."

"So I heard." Part of me should have wished her well and walked off. The other part, the part where my Abuela would have knocked me upside my head and told me to stop being a pendejo had me extending a fucking olive branch. "I can help."

She jerked her head to the side and crossed her arms under her breasts which pushed them up. Frown firmly in place and her eyes were wider than I thought humanly possible. "You can help what?"

"You said your computer imploded. I can help."

She moved her hands down to her hips and tilted her chin with damn near a sneer playing on her lips. "No doubt you spend countless hours battlefield of dutying or whatever, but I hardly think that would make you qualified to offer me 'help'."

I laughed quietly and shook my head. She set that fucking branch aflame then danced on the ashes. Fine. If that's how she wanted to play it.

"You know what, Ma, you're right. My bad. Here I was thinking it might be my degree in Computer Science and my IT/computer repair business of three years."

The haughtiness dissipated and her face paled. I nodded in her direction then turned and walked around the divider. She had to be the most frustrating female I'd ever encountered and that's saying a shit ton considering my sisters and their friends who made ball-busting a fucking Olympic sport. Whatever, I was not going to let her pissy attitude ruin my night. Burgers, beer and soccer.

No sooner than I had gotten settled than did a knock come at my patio door. Ma stood with her computer in hand and hopefully ready to eat crow. I muted the TV, set my plate down, and picked up my beer on my way over to the slider. For half a second I thought about simply pulling the blinds closed in her face, but I could be the bigger person. Maybe.

I opened the door wide enough to lean against the frame,

but not enough that it could be seen as an invitation to enter. I took a slow pull from the bottle before addressing her. "Yes?"

"Lana."

"Excuse me?"

"My name. It's Lana so you can quit calling me Ma or whatever. Though with how you refuse to use Yoda's..."

"Do you understand how an apology is supposed to work?" I asked, cutting her off. She seriously couldn't help herself.

Lana's face filled with color. She really needed to get that under control. She'd suck at poker.

"Yes, right. Sorry." She looked down at her laptop, took a breath, then glanced back up at me. "I was rude. Unnecessarily rude, and for that I apologize."

"Well, shit. That almost sounded sincere."

She frowned. "It was. Is. You were being nice-ish, to offer help. And I shouldn't have been flippant about that."

"Nice-ish?" Again, pressing her buttons was too damn easy as evident in the huff and deepened frown on her face.

"What the hell do you want me to do? Get on my knees and worship you as the great computer god?" The widening of her eyes let me know she knew she'd promptly shoved her foot back into her mouth.

"Later," I replied with a wink. I pushed the door open wider and extended my arm. "Welcome to Casa de Emilio."

Lana hesitated before stepping over the threshold, cradling her laptop to her chest. Her now sadly bra-covered chest. At least she still wore the shorts.

5

LANA

EMILIO CLOSED THE DOOR AND WALKED PAST ME TO RESUME HIS seat. I stood there, clutching my laptop and looking around. I couldn't believe I'd actually come here. To he-who-annoys-me because I needed help. *His* help. Help he'd offered after I'd been rude to him.

He kept his eyes on the silent big screen mounted on the wall and ate his burger. A burger he'd said Yoda was begging for. His thick mass of dark curls hung free around his shoulders. In the times I'd seen him, he'd always had it up, but holy fuck with it down, panties probably melted on sight. I shifted my weight, desperate to ignore how my own were trying to spontaneously combust. *Focus Lana. He's not your type. You like practical. Analytical. Safe. Not chaos.*

"So," he started, "what's wrong with it? You been watching porn and got yourself a virus?"

"What?" I squeaked "No. Who the hell does that?"

He took a drink and smiled. "More people than you'd think. Want one?" He tilted the bottle in my direction.

"No thank you." I looked around again. I needed to focus on anything but the man giving off way too many inappropriate vibes. No watching him chew, or lick his lips to catch a drop of ketchup. *Diversion.* "Your place is surprisingly clean." I inwardly cringed the moment the words slipped out.

He briefly glanced over at me but didn't say anything. Numbers. Numbers I could do. People not so much. Evident in the fact that the happy hour after work invites only extended my way if I happened to overhear the plans being discussed. Too direct. No small talk. Standoff-ish. My lack of people skills garnered me pity invites out of obligation. But I wasn't at work to make friends, so I didn't let it bother me. Too much. Just like I wouldn't let this man bother me. I didn't need to be friends with him, but I could at least attempt to be pleasant all things considering.

Emilio finished his meal, took his plate to the kitchen, and returned, walking right up to me close enough I had to tilt my head to look at him. I licked my lips. My mouth went dry and all the naughty thoughts from earlier played on repeat in my head. *Him.* I could do him. *Shit. What? No!*

"I'm going to pretend you didn't just insult me, again, while still needing my help."

"Sorry, it wasn't meant as an insult. Really. It's just most of the guys I've interacted with at work and personally aren't always as tidy."

"Fair enough. If you met my parents and grandmothers, you'd understand."

His full lips pulled into a genuine smile, revealing a set of pearly whites, and his deep dimples. Those dark eyes of his sparkled and my attention was again drawn to the long lashes. Lucky bastard.

"So, Ma, I need to earn some on your knees, computer god worshipping action." He held his hand out, and I relinquished my laptop while pointedly ignoring his comment.

Emilio opened the lid as he headed back to the sofa. This

time I followed, choosing to sit on the end farthest away from him.

"What'd you do to it?" He spoke without looking in my direction as he typed in things that brought up commands.

"Nothing. It, um, worked fine yesterday but when I went to do some work a little bit ago I had that blue screen of death. But, oh, it had one of those system updates you can't bypass."

He nodded. "Have you backed up?"

"Backed what up?"

He turned his head toward me. His gaze traveled the length of my body then back up to my face. An action I should have found distasteful, but for some odd reason, I was flattered he blatantly checked me out.

"Your files."

"Oh, um, my company has a server thing I think. Something that is supposed to handle all of that."

"How often?"

"What do you mean?"

"How often does it do an auto back up? Hourly? Daily? Weekly? Different services handle it in various ways."

"How the hell am I supposed to know?" I dropped my head forward and pinched the bridge of my nose. "Shit."

He stood and picked up my computer. "It's all good. I got you, Ma." He started walking toward the stairs, and I scrambled behind him.

"Where are you going?"

"My office."

At the top of the stairs, he took a right and walked into a room that made me pause. His office looked like some sort of command center I'd seen on spy shows. A mega console thing with dual monitors was placed against the wall to the right. To the left of it stood one of those tool organizers normally found in a garage. Flanking the other side was a storage rack that held various computers. On the wall by the door was a second smaller desk with a larger, curved monitor that looked more like a small TV and a computer tower that glowed like some sort of sci-fi, space-aged contraption. I'd been desperate when I came over here, and maybe shouldering a little guilt for being bitchy toward him, but, shit, he wasn't playing around.

I took a seat on the edge of the gray futon in the corner, pressed my hands between my knees, and watched him go to work. He put his thick locks up into the man-bun he normally wore and slipped on a pair of glasses. I tilted my head. Why did glasses suddenly make him hotter? I shook off the thought. I needed to stop being distracted by his looks and pray to the universe he could fix my laptop.

A ton of questions sat on my tongue. I wanted to know what he was doing, if it would help and how long it would take. Any time I had to deal with company tech support, everything seemed to take days, if not weeks. Though I suspected they moved slower with me just to be assholes. Either way, I kept quiet.

"You love Pi," he said, breaking the silence for me.

"Huh?"

He indicated toward my shirt. I pulled it away from my body and glanced down.

"Oh. Yeah. Math humor." I added with a shrug.

Emilio swiveled in his chair and stared at me full-on, attention-stealing smile firmly in place, shook his head, and went back to work. Intense and focused. So not what I'd built up in my head as impulsive and chaos. Before I could go too far down that train of thought, he turned, took off his glasses, then linked his arms behind his head, and spread his legs wearing a large grin.

"You are free to start now."

I frowned. "Start what?"

"Your worshipping," he replied with a wink.

I rolled my eyes as I walked toward him. He pushed out of

the way so I could see that he had, in fact, brought it back to life. With all my files intact. "Well, fuck me."

"Okay. I mean I do believe in customer service and all."

I turned just as he whipped his shirt over his head.

My heart rate spiked. "No. Wait. What?"

His hands were on the waistband of his shorts. A sly smile tugged the corner of his mouth upwards. He couldn't be serious.

I narrowed my eyes and crossed my arms. Keeping my hands safely tucked away would stop my desire to trace along the contours of his tattoo. "It's just an expression. Do you go around having sex with all your clients?"

"Nah, you'd be the first."

He ran his tongue along his tempting lips, and I was pretty sure the implication melted my panties. So much, in fact, I damn near checked to see if they were now a puddle around my feet.

This had to be a joke. Some sort of set up. Teasing one step further from the on my knees comment. He had to be messing with me in an attempt to get another rise out of me. Something I hated to admit he did rather easily.

"This could backfire on you," I challenged. My pulse raced and every logical part of my brain said to leave this room and retreat to the safety of my house.

Chaotic. Impulsive. His attitude was leading me down a road I'd never traveled.

He stepped closer. "How so?" The tone of his voice seemed to drop an octave and the laser focus he'd had when working on my computer was now zeroed in on me.

I swallowed the dryness in my mouth and again ignored all logical thinking. "I mean, what if I have to leave a bad review."

"You do seem hard to please," he replied without missing a beat.

I tilted my chin up in defiance. "I have high standards."

Clearly, I was having some sort of out of body experience. What other explanation was there for continuing to entertain any of his notions?

"Well then Ma, lucky for you I take pride in my work and my reputation. I leave no one unsatisfied."

6

EMILIO

LANA'S SIGNATURE FLUSH CREPT UP HER NECK. HONESTLY, I thought she'd have shut this down the minute I took off my shirt, but fuck if she wasn't playing along. Which surprised the hell out of me. I had no idea Ms. Uptight could flirt and be suggestive on purpose. At least where I was concerned. But each reply she gave pushed me to see just how far she'd go in this odd game of chicken.

It was a stare-off. Who would blink first? Her lips twitched to the side and she squared her shoulders and lifted her chin. Then in a move I didn't expect, she took her shirt off and with no hint of a smile anywhere on her face, she took a step forward.

"That's a fairly bold claim."

Sexy Ma was pulling out the big guns, in more ways than one. Alright, I was down with it. I made zero effort to hide the fact I was checking her out.

Her bra was the perfect representation of her. No nonsense. A basic beige, but sheer so I had a full view of her hard, light tan nipples. Freckles decorated her shoulders and across her chest and I felt the need to play connect the dots from one side to the next with my tongue. It took an exorbitant amount of effort for me to not stroke myself because she had my full attention. Wide hips, round ass, and thick thighs, coupled with a perfect handful of tits. Yeah, I was eager as hell to see how far she'd take it.

Ma had called my bluff, raised the stakes. Maybe she wouldn't be so crappy at poker after all. No problem. Hooking my thumbs into the waistband of my shorts, I tugged them down. Her eyes doubled in size as I stood before her with a smile and a raging erection barely hidden behind my boxer briefs. I'd thought about dropping those too, but she had the next move.

"Not a claim, Ma. A fact."

Like when I'd been in her garage, her attention lingered on my dick. She even licked her lips, though I doubted she registered the action. My uptight, passive-aggressive, fine ass neighbor had a little thirst. One I was more than happy to quench.

She took in a long breath before looking back up at me. In damn near slow motion, she tilted her head and drew her top lip in between her teeth. Yeah, Ms. Uptight wasn't ready. She'd be grabbing her shirt and laptop and running out any second now. I took a step back to give her room for the soon-to-be exit.

"Not exactly something I can check on Yelp." She moved closer, erasing the space I'd given her. "Only one way to know for sure."

Well shit, she wasn't backing down. Before I could even say a word, Lana had her hands on either side of my face pulling me down for a kiss. The shock of her actions wore off quickly and I slid my hands around her back to grab her plump ass. She took total control, thrusting her tongue forward while pressing her body close. I gave it back just as hard, reveling in her soft sweetness. She gyrated against me. Her fingers grabbed at the back of my neck. I held her tight, mouths working hard and fast. My cock throbbed between us.

She pulled back and licked her lips. Her chest rose and fell, the action scraping her nipples across my bare torso. "Not bad."

I laughed. Damn, she could cut a man to the quick. "Just 'not bad'?"

She responded with a one-shoulder shrug.

"I believe in five-star service." I leaned down and hesitated to see if she'd stop me.

When she didn't, I placed my hands on either side of her face and ran stroked her cheeks with my thumbs. Our gazes held for one moment. A low sigh flowed from her lips as she parted them slightly.

"Not bad" my ass. Ma wanted more, and that's what she'd get. A peck to the tip of her nose. Followed by a soft kiss to the right corner of her mouth then one to the left side. Finally, I nipped her chin. My forehead rested against hers. She closed her eyes and tilted her chin up. *"Not bad."* She'd be eating her words, even if this went no further.

When I ran my tongue along her bottom lip, she opened her mouth more. I smiled before making a full connection. Slow and smooth. No tongue action. When she tried for more, I pulled back and she gave chase. Lana gripped my arms. I moved one hand behind her neck, the other to her waist.

She whimpered and eagerly pushed forward, clearly not happy with my slower pace. I smiled, before giving her what she wanted. I slipped my tongue in and she moaned in thanks. Lana melted against me, wrapping her arms around my neck, but let me control the pace.

Damn, it'd been a minute since I'd kissed a woman this long and this deep. The feel of her in my arms, her soft body pressed against mine, and the faint sweet scent of cocoa butter all worked together urging me to drag this out as long as possible. Was I still trying to just prove a point? Ma was somehow flipping the script, and if she kept moving like she was I'd need to jerk off and still take a cold shower afterward.

Abandoning her mouth, I ran my nose along her jawline and lightly nipped at her earlobe. "Ready to amend your assessment?" I whispered.

I pulled back to get a better look at her. Her face was flushed, her breathing heavy, and nipples diamond-hard.

She sank her teeth into her bottom lip before she broke out into a smile. "It would seem I was wrong." She stopped and ran her pointer finger down my chest until she got to the waistband of my boxers. "But...you've not completed the job."

Aww shit now. She was full of surprises. When she glanced up at me, the look on her face was something between lust and a little uncertainty. Nah, if she wanted this game to continue, she'd have to make the next move. I took three steps back and spread my arms wide.

"If you're feeling froggy, Ma. Then you best jump now."

She frowned. "What the hell does that mean?"

"It means I got condoms and time."

She crossed her arms and tapped her finger against her mouth. Her gaze dropped to my aching dick then she took a breath and smiled wide. Gaze locked on mine, she lowered her shorts.

"Ribbit."

7

LANA

HOLY SHIT DID I SAY THAT? THE BROAD SMILE ON EMILIO'S FACE indicated I had in fact lost all my senses. But damn, that kiss, not to mention the thickness hiding behind the thin boxer briefs he wore. And the fact he seemed to be into me. How the hell did I go from thinking he was the most annoying person on the planet to standing in just my underwear ready to jump his bones?

He held his hand out toward me and I slipped mine in. I followed him from the command center, down the hall to the double door entrance of his bedroom. All the while thinking of the things I'd hoped he'd do to me because if he could kiss like that, then what other magical things could he do with his tongue?

When he let go, the emptiness was instant. I kept my attention on his ass as he walked over to his single nightstand to the right of his king-sized bed. What was I doing? Was I really about to have sex with a man I barely knew and couldn't say with certainty I even liked?

Emilio pulled out a row of condoms, set them on the

wooden surface then dropped his briefs. My mouth went dry and his exposed dick acted as a magnet to my tingling pussy.

Yes. The answer was yes. Yes I was. And I was going to enjoy the hell out of it. Hopefully.

Onto the bed he went. Arms behind his head, legs spread wide, erection at attention and ready for action.

"All yours, Ma."

I tilted my head. "You're the one with something to prove. Shouldn't you be working harder to seduce me?"

He smiled, licked those magnificent lips, and started stroking himself. His hand went down and back up with a gentle twist of his wrist. Down again, back up and then a slow circle over the darker head. "Ma, you're in my room, wearing nothing but your underwear, and watching me like a thirsty woman starin' down a glass of ice water. I'd say you're plenty seduced."

I swallowed hard and tried not to visibly shudder at his cocky words. The dampness between my legs was undeniable and the friction of my nipples against the fabric of my bra acted as micro torture. That and the fact he wasn't crowding me. He seemed in no hurry to "seal the deal" as it were. And damn if his hands-off approach wasn't somehow both sweet and annoyingly fucking effective in making me want him more.

He maintained eye contact while continuing to pleasure himself. I'd never watched a man masturbate, but damn if it wasn't a mesmerizing sight. Part of me wanted to let him continue, but another part of me was inexplicably jealous that his hand was on himself and not me.

"Again with more hot air. It takes more than the sight of a big dick to get me in the mood."

The bastard laughed. He stopped his action and inched to the foot of the bed then made the come here motion. As if on an invisible string, I glided toward him. Once in reach, he placed his warm hands on my waist and leaned forward to place a soft kiss on my stomach. I gripped his shoulders to steady myself.

Emilio looked up at me as he ran his hands down my hips and across until his thumbs met in the center. Gracious, when had eye contact become such a turn on? Or maybe it was just him, and the disarming, laser focus he emitted. Eyes never leaving my face, he stroked ever so softly up and down over my thin panties, no doubt feeling the evidence of my lie.

"You're overdressed."

I ran my tongue along the back of my teeth. "Well, maybe you should take some initiative and rectify that situation."

Without a word, he rose to full height and in mere seconds I was liberated of my bra.

I arched a brow. "Done that a time or two?"

A sly smile tugged at the corner of his mouth. "Told you, Ma, I'm good at what I do."

Maneuvering so he stood behind me, Emilio moved my hair to the side and placed a kiss below my ear. "Shall I keep going?"

I swallowed and nodded. His hard cock pressed against my back as he slowly glided his hands along my sides, creating goosebumps at the feather-light sensation and my eyes reflexively closed as a soft moan escaped.

A warm burst of air wafted across my heated flesh when he let out a low chuckle. Emilio continued his languid exploration. A frustrating tease of touching, but not, ignoring all the parts of my body that desperately longed for attention. He rolled his hands over the globes of my ass and gave them a firm squeeze before hooking his fingers into my panties and pulling them down. The cotton material gave way to gravity and pooled at my feet. I stepped out of them, flinging them off to the side.

Skin-to-skin. Inhibitions and all logical reasoning discarded like my clothes.

"You good?"

I responded with a breathy "Yes."

I melted into him as one hand danced down my belly and the other slid up to cup my breast. An appreciative moan rumbled in the back of my throat when he rolled my pebbled nipple between his fingertips. My breath stilled as Emilio ran his hand over my pussy. He kissed the side of my neck. I parted my legs to give him more access. Not missing a beat, he spread my folds, and ever so softly made circles on my clit. As if they had a mind of their own, I began rotating my hips to match his touch.

Emilio flicked my earlobe with his tongue before giving it a gentle nip. "How's this, Ma? Properly seduced yet?" His husky tenor caused me to shudder. He pinched my nipple, and I whimpered with delight.

I didn't need to see him to know he probably had that damned smirk on his face. Bastard.

"I...ah..." Shit, I couldn't even talk.

A short gasp escaped when he slid his fingers into my body. With as wet as I was, he met no resistance. I reached back, gripping his neck, and propped a leg up on the bed. He worked me with precision. In and out he moved while his thumb circled my clit. I rocked against his actions, my breathing becoming ragged. The pressure started in my stomach. The exciting build of anticipation. I needed more. Faster. But Emilio was in no hurry. He kept his easy, steady, frustrating pace.

I teetered on the edge, desperate to fall. He stopped working the fingers inside me and instead pressed down on my stiff nub. Concentrated pressure on the bundle of nerves pushed me over. My leg slipped to the floor, and I fell forward, bracing myself on the bed, and letting the bliss wash over me. My body shook and my head swam. I barely registered Emilio had changed position until I felt his mouth on me.

He sat on the floor between my spread legs, his back against the footboard, and hands holding my ass. I stared in amazement as he licked and sucked my sensitive clit. Never before had I watched a guy go down on me, and holy fuck it was the most erotic thing I'd ever witnessed.

I pressed my lips together, closed my eyes, and started rocking back and forth. Christ, the scrape of his beard along my thighs and the flick of his tongue had me spiraling. He massaged and kneaded my butt while he relentlessly worked me over. His skills sure as hell didn't stop at kissing.

He licked a path down my slit, taking his time. I gripped the bed, and my eyes popped open when he closed his lips around my clit and suckled it. He pushed his face closer leaving only the dark curls of his hair visible. My knees buckled and I cried when the second wave hit. He didn't stop. He squeezed my ass and pressed his tongue flat against me, laving my overly stimulated flesh.

My lungs constricted and my body shook. I couldn't handle another one. "Em...Emilio...wait...I need to breathe."

He placed a kiss to one thigh, then the other before wedging himself between me and the bed, forcing me upright as he did. I rested my forehead against his chest and put up no resistance when he turned us so I could lie down.

I draped my arm across my face. "Fuck me," I whispered.

"I'm trying, but you tapped out."

8

EMILIO

I LICKED MY LIPS, TASTING THE SWEETNESS OF LANA THAT remained there, and tried not to smile when she propped up on her elbows and frowned at me. A well-sexed woman was a beautiful sight, and she was exactly that. Her chest continued to rise and fall in exaggerated movements. There was a flush to her face, strands of hair clinging to her damp forehead, and her pussy glistened, wet and ready for more. If she was.

She pursed her lips and let her gaze drop to my damn near painful erection before looking back up at me. "Well, I think you've proven your point...so..." Again her attention went to my cock and a devilish smile took up residence on her face. "I'd say I'm all good."

Alright, that was how it would go. I nodded and started stroking myself. "Whatever you say, Ma. But two things. One, I'm going to enjoy being able to say I told you so every chance I get. And two, something tells me you're the type of woman who thoroughly does her research. So, you'll be back."

Lana's attention remained on my motions. "Is that so?" The slight quiver in her voice betrayed her flippant remark.

I stepped closer. "Yeah."

Her mouth fell open and she pressed her knees together. I leaned against the foot of the bed, closed my eyes and tilted my head back. Inhaling deeply, the lingering scent of her invaded my senses as I stroked myself. My dick ached for relief, and while I'd rather be buried deep between her legs, taking care of myself would have to be a less satisfying consolation prize.

Like a movie on repeat, I mentally flipped through the events of the last hour. The first reveal of her breasts. The feel of her pebbled nipples beneath my thumb. I slid my hand up my length, squeezing the head, before drawing it back. She let out a quiet groan. I kept going. The image of her thick thighs and plump ass flashed in my mind.

Soft skin. I licked my lips again. Damn, she'd tasted good. Down, then up I moved my hand. The memory of her slickness coating my fingers as I had my first exploration inside her body. What I wouldn't have given to have my dick sheathed in her warm heat. There was a shift in the mattress.

Opening my eyes, I watched as Lana inched her way closer until she sat with her legs on either side of me. She didn't touch me but had positioned herself for an up-close and personal viewing. Her face was cock level and if she leaned forward, I could have slipped it between her full lips.

She drew the corner of her bottom one between her teeth and bunched the covers in her fists. Her chest rose and fell in slow controlled breaths matching my own. I kept the motion of my hand slow and steady. She kept her eyes focused on my dick. This might be the single sexiest encounter and I wasn't even going to fuck her. What were the odds of that?

My balls tightened and I knew it wouldn't be much longer. "You...you might want to move back." My heart raced. Relief was knocking at the door.

Instead of moving, Lana reached up and placed her hand atop mine. With our gazes locked, she worked in tandem with me. A gentle tug, then a squeeze. She used her thumb to circle my swollen tip and arched her back, a silent invitation. With a long groan, I couldn't hold back any longer. My release shot forward, splattering her tits and chin before she squealed and turned her head to avoid being hit in the face.

I sped up my movements, the final spurts of my orgasm landing on her with some dribbling down my hand. Spent, I clumsily stumbled forward and collapsed beside her.

"Five stars?"

She wiped her hand across her chest, coating her fingers in my jizz. "A bit messy. Four point five."

I chuckled and pushed off the bed, crossing the room over to the bathroom. I wet a washcloth and returned. Kneeling in front of her, I cleaned her off, leaned forward to give her a peck on the lips, and smiled.

"Five-star service."

She took the rag from my hand. "May I?" she asked, inclining her head toward my bathroom.

"Help yourself, Ma."

I had zero shame in watching the jiggle of her ass as she walked away. This wasn't exactly how I'd planned to spend my evening, but I wasn't complaining.

By the time she returned, I'd redressed and had collected her clothes. The ends of her hair were wet like she'd done a quick wash job.

Jutting her chin in the direction of the bed, Lana looked at the items then over at me. "Trying to get rid of me?"

"Not at all. Just going the extra mile. But you're free to walk around naked. Won't get a single complaint from me. I like the view," I added with a wink.

She twisted her lips from side to side then shook her head and started to dress. "This is so out of the norm for me."

I sat at the foot of the bed. Watching her get dressed wasn't nearly as exciting as her undressing, but I enjoyed the show all the same. "What is?"

"Having sex—though technically we didn't have sex—with someone I don't even like."

My ego didn't even have time to get bruised. No sooner than the words were out, they were followed by a loud gasp and her partially nude body turned bright red.

"Shit. I...I didn't mean it like that. Crap. Crap. Crap. It's just that we've been antagonistic in our interactions up until now. Hell, we didn't even know each other's names before today...so. Shit. I'm sorry."

She kept her head down as she jammed her legs into her shorts. I wanted to be mad or even offended, but it wasn't like she was wrong.

Though the part about not liking me stung. I was a friendly guy. Got along with most people. But from the moment she'd moved in, it'd been eye rolls, frowns, or outright pretending she didn't see me.

"Why is that?"

"Why I don't go around getting naked with people that I haven't had positive interactions with prior?"

I chuckled softly and combed my fingers through my hair. "Uh, no. Why don't you like me?"

She stopped mid-pull before finally lowering her shirt down and lifting her hair that had gotten trapped. Her eyes widened and she puffed out her cheeks. "Oh."

"Yeah, oh. I think it's a valid question. All things considering."

She ran her hand down her neck and licked her lips. Lips I wouldn't mind having more quality time with.

"Can I have a glass of water?"

I let out a short laugh and nodded. "Smooth stall tactic, but sure." Pushing off the bed, I headed out the door, but stopped and turned back. "Feel free to grab your computer."

"Um...what do I owe you?"

I smiled. "I'll bill ya later."

She had her laptop cradled against her breasts when she entered the kitchen. "Thanks," she said, taking the glass from my hand. "And it's not a stall tactic."

I rested back against the counter, crossed my ankles and folded my arms over my chest, and waited. She stared at the ice cubes in her glass before taking a drink. Setting both it and the computer down, she looked around my place before settling her eyes back on me.

"This," she said, stretching her arms out wide.

"This what?" I glanced around the room trying to figure out what the hell she was alluding to.

"This unit. I wanted it but before I could weigh all the pros and cons you swooped in and bought it."

I blinked once. Twice. No way I'd heard Ma correctly. "Come again?"

She huffed and put her hands on her hips. "I wanted the end unit. That way I'd only have to share one wall. But I needed to make sure this was the best choice, so I had to lay out the pros and cons of this unit compared to the other two I was deciding on."

I rose to full height and frowned at her. "How in the hell is your indecisiveness my fault? And it's not like this was the last end unit."

She stomped toward me wearing her favorite facial expression. "I'm not indecisive, I'm conscientious. A major purchase, like buying a house, takes some thinking to make sure it's the right choice. Who does things like that all willy-nilly?"

Shit, she was serious. I laughed. Hard and deep, I laughed.

The scowl on her face deepened. "I don't see what's so funny."

I wiped imaginary tears from my eyes. "You, Ma. You're hysterical. First, 'willy-nilly' seriously? More like I'm a man that knows what he likes and goes for it." I gave her an appreciative glance to prove my point. "Second, you've been harboring resentment toward me for something that was totally of your own making."

She opened her mouth but closed it again without saying anything. With a deep inhale and slow exhale, Lana swiped her laptop from the counter. "Thanks for fixing it." She turned on her heel and stalked toward the slider.

I thought about stopping her but didn't see the point.

9

LANA

I SAT AT MY KITCHEN TABLE EYEING THE DECORATIVE TIN OF cookies.

"Why am I doing this, Yoda?" His lack of acknowledgment at his name being called was answer enough to my rhetorical question.

An olive branch, or apology, or both wrapped up in cookie goodness.

"Ugh!" I groaned and dropped my head onto the table. I'd stormed out of his place two days ago and had luckily been able to not see him, even in passing, since then.

He'd been right.

I hated that he'd been right.

Sure, he was annoying in some ways, but my level of hostility toward him wasn't all because of his actions. And goodness, I'd acted that way after he'd fixed my computer and...my body heated simply thinking about our sexual encounter. Damn, his mouth was good for more than making smart-ass comments. So much more. Emilio had totally wiped me out and we hadn't made it to the actual sex.

I groaned again. Yet another thing he'd been right about. I

was curious, so fucking curious about how good he'd actually be. And my every instinct told me I'd be eating way more crow in that regard than I was about to for the upcoming apology.

Scratching at my leg caused me to look down. Yoda whimpered, then sat, and I leaned to pick him up. He spent a good bit of time channeling a cat level of aloofness, but he did offer up the grace of his presence when I needed it the most. Like now.

"I can do this, buddy. I'm an adult that can own up to being wrong." He leaned back in my arms, presenting his belly for proper rubs.

For two days I'd thought about the enigma of the man next door. Annoying, but helpful. Funny, and sexy. And talented. So very talented in so many ways. A smile pulled at my lips as I mentally cataloged everything he'd done and wondered what more he could do. And though I was damn near loathed to admit it—even to myself—hanging out with Emilio could be somewhat pleasant. When he wasn't being overly cocky.

"Okay," I said setting Yoda back on the floor. "Don't throw any wild ragers while I'm next door." He trotted off, jumped onto the couch and promptly curled up on his favorite blanket.

I grabbed the tin from the table and padded down the hall toward my front door, stopping to slide on a pair of flip flops. The ten-second walk to Emilio's had my stomach in knots. Why in the hell was apologizing to him making me all nervous?

I rang the bell. No answer. His door had a thin sidelight and as I peered through I saw no movement. I rang the bell again. Figures. I'd finally come over and he wasn't even home. I couldn't stop the laugh that started. What was it about him that made me blame him for everything? Taking a breath, I shook my head and got my giggles under control.

The deep roar of an engine stole my attention. Barreling down the street at a speed too fast for the narrow passageway, was a shiny deep black old school muscle car. The type I associated with guys who had way too much testosterone that I was sure had them overcompensating for other things. The metallic air intake thing protruding from the hood gleamed in the sunlight as the monstrous car closed in. The driver crawled to a stop and peered at me before breaking out into a large grin. I jumped when the garage of his unit rumbled to life and he eased the pristine vehicle into the driveway.

I hugged the tin container against my abdomen. However, I knew for a fact he was not overcompensating for a damn thing. My face heated at the thought. The silence of the engine followed by the slam of a door made me look in his direction.

"What can I do for ya, Ma?" He leaned lazily against the car and crossed his arms in front of his chest. Cocky smirk firmly in place on his heavenly lips.

That name. Damned if it wasn't annoying and unexplainably arousing at the same time. The grin on his face got bigger.

"Took you longer than I expected to come back for another taste, but your crap-ass poker face is giving you away. Come on in, and I'll hook you up."

The wink at the end of the statement flamed indignation at him being so pompous and presumptuous. And right. Damn it all to hell.

Ignoring that fact, I lifted my chin and drew my brows together. Stretching to pull every inch I could out of my height I squared my shoulders and glared at him. "Slow your roll, buddy. I only came to make a peace offering, but not sure I will now.

He laughed. Outright laughed as he turned his back to me and headed into the house with me fast on his heels.

"Only you would renege on a peace offering. So, what, pray tell, am I not getting?" He called out over his shoulder.

Emilio waited patiently for me to cross his threshold before he shut the door. He dropped his keys and wallet on a small side table and continued down the hall as if me being there and annoyed by him was an everyday occurrence. Into the kitchen and straight to the fridge. He pulled out two beers, popped the tops off both and handed me one. I didn't miss the smile on his face as he tipped his to his lips.

I set the tin on the counter and gave it a push so it slid towards him. "Cookies."

His eyes widened and I took a drink of the beer to cover the laugh threatening to escape. He put his down and picked up the offering.

"You...baked me cookies?" He opened the lid and inhaled before pulling one free. The sweet treat was suspended mid-air in front of his mouth. "Wait, did you poison these?"

I took another pull from my bottle and kept my gaze leveled at him. "You really believe me capable of that?"

"Without a doubt," he replied, then took a giant bite.

The drink I'd just taken ungraciously sputtered past my lips and dribbled down my chin as I choked on a laugh.

He finished his cookie and licked his lips while handing me a paper towel. "You good?"

I nodded and cleaned my face. "Why would you do that?"

"Do what?" He nabbed another cookie from the tin.

I focused on the treat then looked up at him. "Eat something you thought was poisoned?"

He grabbed the tin and his beer and headed toward his living room. "Eh, there are worse ways to go, Ma. Besides, it's bad manners to turn your nose up at a gift."

Emilio settled his long limbs on his couch, put down the tin, picked up the remote, then patted the space next to him. Silently I complied with his unspoken request.

"I'm waiting," he said, keeping his eyes firmly on the TV.

"Waiting for what?"

He turned to look at me and gave me a total body once over before his attention settled back on my face. "The apology that goes along with those delicious cookies."

I faced him and crossed my arms. "Who said I was apologizing?"

The side of his mouth kicked up into a half-smile. "You did when you were standing outside my door looking like a creeper and holding a tin of baked goodies." He reached forward and retrieved another cookie to make his point.

I shot up from my reclined position. "I was not looking like a...a 'creeper.' You act as if you caught me peeping in your windows or something. I rang the bell, like a normal human. I was leaving when you came roaring down the street in your obnoxiously loud car."

Emilio laughed. Deep, rich, and hard. A laugh that should have pissed me off, but instead rolled over me like warm caramel. Damn it, how did he manage to annoy and yet put me at ease all at the same time?

"Relax, Ma. Have a cookie. It'll make you feel better." He leaned closer and licked his lips. "Unless you want to work out some of that stress some other way."

Gracious be, he was close. And tempting. His mouth. Yes! Everything in me screamed yes, but I refused to give him the satisfaction. I moved forward. His smile broadened. I licked my lips. His Adam's apple bobbled. Closer.

"A cookie will do." I smiled as I leaned back with my prize in hand.

Confusion sparkled in his dark eyes before amusement took over. "Suit yourself, Ma."

I chomped down on my treat but didn't taste any of the sweet goodness. It was a poor substitution for what I actually wanted.

"How's your computer?"

"It's good. And I brought an external hard drive thingy to back up stuff."

He chuckled under his breath and took a swig from his beer. "'Thingy' that's..." He stopped talking when he saw the frown on my face. Emilio cleared his throat. "Let me know if you need any help."

"Why? Another excuse to get me over here?"

He arched a brow. "Hate to break it to you, Ma, but I've not had to use a single excuse. You've come knockin' at my door all on your own."

I closed my eyes and took a slow breath. Damn if I didn't walk right into that. "I guess you'd be correct there."

"You guess? Damn, Ma. What do you do?"

"Huh?"

"That job you stressed that *some* people had."

I inwardly cringed remembering that statement. "Oh...um I'm an Accounts Payable Manager. Why?"

"Cuz, I'm trying to figure out what in your daily life makes it so hard to admit when you're wrong."

Once again his offhand comment flamed my indignation. "I wasn't wrong."

He stood and grabbed both empty beer bottles. "Well, you sure as hell wasn't right. Want another?"

I pressed my palms against my eyes and shook my head. The heat creeping up my neck let me know that it was probably bright red, a shining beacon of my frustration. I'd come over here to apologize and being around him threw all those intentions out the window.

Pushing off the couch, I ambled down the hall for a goodbye and to go home before I shoved my other foot into my mouth. "So...enjoy your cookies, I'm going to head out."

Emilio shut the fridge door and turned. "Running out before I get my apology."

"Why are you hung up on that?"

"Why are you avoiding it?"

"I'm not."

He placed the bottle on the counter then hopped up and took a seat. "You are, but it's okay, Ma. Your secret is safe with me." He winked before picking up his beer and taking a drink.

I rolled my eyes at the continued use of the freaking moniker he insisted on calling me, and stepped forward, challenging his nonsensical statement. "What secret?"

"The fact you have to hang on to something so you have a reason to come back." He licked his lips and smiled.

Smug bastard.

10

EMILIO

PUSHING HER BUTTONS WAS ALMOST TOO EASY. MA WAS WAY TOO
high-strung and needed to learn to relax and simply enjoy life.
As annoying as her somewhat uppity attitude could be, the
peeks at the free spirit clawing to get out had me enjoying her
random visits.

She crossed her arms and pushed her lips into a pout while
frowning at me. "You are awfully full of yourself."

I eased off the countertop and stepped to her. "Play your
cards right, Ma, and you can be full of me."

Her eyes widened and she dropped her arms to her side. I
advanced and she moved backward until she hit the wall. She
tilted her chin up to look at me and rolled her tongue along her
bottom lip.

"You're a cocky jerk. I'm not sure I like you." Her words were
delivered with a lot less bite than she probably hoped for.

I ran my thumb across her cheek and leaned closer to her
ear. "You like me well enough to get you off, let's start there."

Ma sucked in a quick breath and snapped her head to the
side. With our faces inches from each other, I waited to hear
what smart ass thing she'd have to say next. Instead, she

connected her mouth with mine. Her hands clenched my shirt as she pulled our bodies together.

I thrust my tongue forward as I pushed her against the wall, my hand at her throat keeping her in place as I drowned myself in the kiss. She moaned, giving as good as she got while rubbing herself along my dick which was quickly growing hard from the contact. I broke away from her soft lips and nipped along her jaw. Her warm hands ran up my back beneath my shirt.

Continuing to kiss the side of her neck, I licked and suckled the soft flesh while letting my fingers journey south. I stroked her through the thin leggings she wore which elicited another low moan from her.

"Tell me whatcha want, Ma," I whispered before gently grabbing her lobe between my teeth.

She responded by pushing her hips forward, her nails dug into my back. I made a tsking sound.

Her breath caught when I slipped my hand inside her pants. The dampness of her panties brought forth the memory of how sweet she'd tasted. My mouth watered for more.

"You can do better than that. Use your words."

This path could easily blow up in my face and leave me with a major case of blue balls if she walked out. Hell, as much as I teased her, I wanted to take things to a different completion. The next time I came with this woman, I wanted it to be while balls deep inside her. My dick throbbed at the thought.

I continued my teasing, reveling in the increased wetness of her underwear. Sliding my other hand up her neck, I ran my thumb across her bottom lip. She responded by opening her mouth and letting her tongue swirl around the digit. A simple thing, but damn did it make me wish it was my cock and not a finger getting that treatment.

"Whatcha say, Ma? Wanna find out just how good it can be?"

Her breathing changed and her eyes half-closed. "Ye...yes. Fuck yes."

My mouth descended on hers again. I moved the thin barrier to the side and easily slipped two fingers into her pussy. A little pressure applied to her clit, she rocked her hips in sync with my hand and I swallowed down the low cry that accompanied her release. I kept stroking her and her nails dug into my back creating the most pleasurable pain. I'd wear the scratches left behind as a fucking badge of honor.

Lana rested her head back against the wall. A post-coital flush colored her skin. With a final swipe, I pulled my hand free and stepped back to admire her relaxed posture. Reaching to the right, I pulled open the small drawer and retrieved a row of condoms.

She tilted her head and narrowed her eyes. "You keep condoms in your kitchen?"

I winked at her. "I'm like a boy scout. Always prepared." Slipping my arm around her waist, I pulled her to me and headed back to the living room. "Time for a ride, Ma."

"A ride? Where are we going?"

I stopped in front of my couch, dropped the packets on the table, and let her go before pushing down my shorts. Her eyes widened and her lips formed a silent "O." She stepped closer and wrapped her warm hands around my neglected dick. The sensation of her gentle caress had me groaning. I closed my eyes, enjoying the softness of her touch. She kissed my chin and down the front of my neck, all the while continuing the slow strokes.

"I can't ride standing up," she whispered between kisses. She let go and stepped back, a coy smile on her face as she started removing her clothes.

I tugged my shirt over my head and kicked my pants free and took a seat. Thick and sexy, Lana stood between my legs in a sheer white panty and bra set, one that was just as utilitarian as the last set I'd seen her in. Her puckered light tan nipples peeked out from behind the thin fabric.

The damp spot on her panties was damn near eye level. My cock twitched at the sight. I slid forward and ran my hands up the curve of her hips. With a slight tug, she stumbled closer, putting her hands on my shoulders to brace herself. I pressed my lips against her pussy, inhaling her intoxicating scent while getting a taste of her sweetness all at the same time.

She dug her fingers into my shoulder and propped one leg up onto the sofa. I gripped her hips, pulling her closer as I teased her through the thin cotton barrier. She gyrated against me, her fingers tangled in my hair, holding me in place as she controlled the pressure. Damn, I loved a woman who knew what she wanted.

My dick ached from need. As if reading my mind, Lana pushed me back. With a sexy smile, she wiggled out of her panties before making quick work of removing her bra. She stood before me gloriously naked and sexy as fuck.

Reaching down, she grabbed one of the condoms and kept her eyes on me as she opened it. Slowly she lowered to her knees and took hold of my cock at the base. A move that made me groan and lift my hips. She gave it a gentle squeeze and ran her hand up my length, circling the tip with her thumb. Fuck what I wouldn't give for her to wrap those full lips around me, but as she started rolling the condom on, I knew that wasn't in the cards tonight. Next time.

There definitely needed to be a next time because I needed more of her. Not just the sex though, her, all of her. The smart ass mouth, eye rolls, and hell even the condescension in her voice which had an odd adorable factor to it.

She rose, pussy glistening and moved to straddle me. With my dick poised at her entrance she paused. "You know if this isn't the ride of my life I'll never let you live it down."

I put my hands on her waist and pulled her down just enough to slip the tip in. "Satisfaction guaranteed, Ma."

Lana leaned forward, placed her hands on either side of my face and kissed me while lowering herself, but not all the way. Her tongue probed my mouth and I grabbed her soft ass, squeezing the tender flesh. Up she went again until I nearly popped out of her, then down again. Fuck this tease would be the death of me, but I resisted the urge to rush her process. Instead, I leaned my head against the back of the sofa and concentrated on falling into the pace she set. Up and when she lowered this time, she enveloped me completely.

She gripped my shoulders and let out a breath.

"You good, Ma?"

She nodded. "It's not like I hadn't seen it, but...big things are hidden in skinny packages."

It was probably not the best time, but I couldn't help but laugh. "I mean, I did say you'd be full of me, emphasis on the full."

With my arms around her waist, I lifted my hips, burying myself deeper. Her sharp gasp drove me wild. I pressed my lips against her neck and thrust upward again on a mission to elicit every sound of pleasure she offered.

"Fuck," she groaned.

Lana shifted, rising up onto her knees and took hold of the back of the sofa. Her tits dangled in my face, an offering I couldn't ignore. I squeezed the soft flesh, bringing it to my mouth. I flicked my tongue across her hardened nipple. Ma rocked her hips back and forth and the sensation of her sliding along my stiff dick was nothing short of exceptional.

She arched her back, pushing her breasts against my face as she continued to move. I shifted my attention from one tit to the next. The nights I'd spent fantasizing about this moment were nothing compared to actually having her ride me hard. I dropped my head onto the back of the sofa and let my hand wander down her waist and around to her plump ass. I gave it a smack. She looked down at me and I smiled.

Lifting my hips, I matched her stroke for stroke. Ma moved faster. Mouth open, eyes narrowed to mere slits, and low, breathy moans poured free with each thrust. My balls tightened and I knew it wouldn't be much longer before I lost my load. I slipped a hand between our bodies, finding the hidden treasure I was after. Pressing my fingers against her clit, I rubbed in quick circles as she dug her fingers into my shoulders.

"Holy fuck," she groaned before she clenched around me.

I grabbed her ass and pumped upwards and grunted as I filled the condom with my own release. Lana rested her head on me, her hot breath coming out in quick spurts. I wrapped my arms around her waist and held her as we both came down.

Ma lifted up and eased herself off me to sit on the cushion to my right. "It's rather annoying you keep being right."

I leaned over and kissed her cheek. "Told you, Ma. Satisfaction guaranteed."

11

LANA

"Ugh, this is useless," I said to Yoda and shut the lid of my laptop.

He didn't even perk his ears up to acknowledge I'd spoken. Brat. He was a brat, but he was my brat and I loved him. Reaching over, I rubbed his fur to calm my nerves.

It was simply sex. Great sex. Amazing sex. The kind of sex that other people had, not me. Until Emilio. And I wanted more.

But it was a bad idea. A terrible idea.

A one-off was fine. Anything more than that and things could get complicated. This was worse than fraternizing with a co-worker which was strictly a no-go. That kind of thing was messy and avoiding messy was what I did best.

"Maybe I should make a pros and cons list." I looked over at Yoda who again failed to even acknowledge I'd spoken to him. "You know, I feed you, bathe you, clothe you, and give you a place to live. The least you can do is look in my direction when I'm talking to you."

This time his ears at least twitched. Guess it was better than nothing. I picked up the remote and readjusted to a more comfortable position on the couch. If I couldn't get work done, bingeing old episodes of *Law and Order* would be the next best thing. Yoda popped his head up, then jumped off the couch, barking as he ran full steam toward the front door. Seconds later the doorbell chimed.

"Who in the hell?" I groaned, unfolding myself from my position. I'd just gotten settled. "Stop with the noise," I scolded as I got closer. "You act as if you've never heard the doorbell before."

A quick look through the peephole made my breath catch. Damn it all to hell, I'd talked him up. I did a slow exhale and put on my best annoyed face. Yoda darted out the small opening and jumped at Emilio's ankles. *Traitor.*

"You have crappy timing."

The friendly smile he wore quickly turned into a frown. "Damn, I can't get a hello before you start bitching at me?"

I crossed my arms and leaned against the door. "You're right. Sorry. Hello. And you have crappy timing. I'd just gotten comfortable and here you come to mess it up."

He laughed and bent down to pick up Yoda, the brown plastic bag in his hand rustling as he did. "Is she this pissy with everyone, Ren, or is it just me?"

I rolled my eyes at the dumb name he insisted on calling Yoda and reached out to take him. "What can I say, you bring out the best in me."

His grin got wider and I worked to ignore the effect it had on me. Emilio sauntered in without waiting for an invitation.

"So, what were you doing that I rudely interrupted by giving you the pleasure of my company?"

I shut the door and set Yoda down. He ran back to the living room probably to reclaim his favorite spot on the couch.

"Pleasure? That might be a stretch."

Emilio turned to stare at me. Those dark brown eyes, framed by the black full lashes, and the smirk firmly planted on his lips called me on my bullshit without him having to say a word.

I cleared my throat and shoved my hands in my pockets to keep from fanning myself. "Anyway, what brings you over?"

He held up the bag. "Being a good neighbor and returning your container. Figured it'd be easier on you to have the same one for next time."

"Excuse me? Next time? Who the hell said anything about a next time?"

When I grabbed for the bag, he wrapped his hand around my wrist and pulled me against his body.

"Awww, Ma, you wouldn't do me like that would you? Give me a taste of your sweet, sweet treats and not let me have more. And here I was thinking you were starting to like me just a little."

He licked his lips and I damn near moaned. His words were smooth and easy. The low, throaty tenor of his voice only added to the dirty innuendo hidden in his message. The burn of wanton desire spiraled around me hot and fast and I clenched against the pulsating between my legs.

My mouth went dry and my brain turned to mush, preventing me from giving him a witty comeback. *Damn him! Damn him straight to hell.* Never in my life had a man gotten under my skin as much as he did. And never had I enjoyed the frustration of it like I did with him. Our own sort of foreplay. And boy did it have an effect. I pulled back and attempted to pay no attention to the newfound dampness of my panties.

"We'll have to do something about that," I said, turning to head toward my kitchen.

"Do something about what?" His voice boomed from behind as he followed me.

"You thinking I like you."

He laughed at me again. I set the bag on the counter and

turned, planting my hands on my hips and the most indignant look I could muster on my face.

"And why is that funny? An excellent roll in the hay does not constitute me liking you."

A full smile spread across his face putting his pearly whites on display. He rubbed his hands together and I mentally kicked myself for the inflation to his ego.

"Ma, come on now. You just love to tell on yourself. It's kinda cute actually. But I'll play. If two '*excellent* rolls in the hay' plus home-baked goods don't constitute you liking me, what does? A third? Because I'm game."

"Your math seems to be off. Or you're getting me confused with someone." For some reason that thought annoyed me and I refused to give myself time to analyze why.

"I know who I'm talking about. We may not have bumped uglies that first time, but getting you off more than once counts in my book."

I drew my brows together and tilted my head. "Bumped what?"

He let out an overly dramatic sigh. "Bumped uglies. Knocked boots. Did a little bump and grind..." He did a suggestive roll of his hips that finished off with two quick thrusts and I did my best to not let my gaze linger too long on his crotch.

"Oh...why the hell can't you just say had sex?"

He leaned his lanky form against the doorframe and crossed his arms, wearing another disarmingly attractive grin. "Where's the fun in that?"

I covered my face and groaned. One rash decision after the next embedded this man deeper and deeper into my life. "Fine. Wait...is that why you really came over here? Hoping for another hookup?"

"Nope." He added an extra pop to the "P" when he said the word. "I legit just came to bring your container back like the great neighbor that I am." He pushed off the wall and closed the space between us. "But if you're feening I'm more than happy to help you out."

"Me? You're the one who took the turn down sexual lane." A smile tugged at my lips. "Maybe...maybe you're the one really 'feening' and are trying to put it off on me."

I managed to hold not only my composure but also his eye contact during my bullshit statement. Although, possibly not all bullshit. There had to be some part, other than the obvious one, that was attracted to me.

He rolled his tongue along his bottom lip before drawing it in between his teeth. "If I am, you gonna let me get a fix?"

Emilio stood close but didn't touch me. And damn if I didn't want him to have his hands, lips, and tongue all over me. This man was everything I normally avoided. Crude, slightly arrogant, and spoke sarcasm like it was a second language. Yet I was ready to take him by the hand and drag him upstairs. Because he was also funny, intelligent, and super laid back, which was the yin to my high-strung yang.

"You come prepared?"

He slowly shook his head.

I arched a brow. "Thought you were Mr. Boy Scout?"

He quirked the right side of his mouth up. "Need me to run home?"

Hell no. But I kept that thought to myself. Letting him walk out that door might have me losing my nerve and not let him back in.

I stepped forward and wrapped my arms around his neck. "Lucky for you I was a girl scout. We too know to be prepared."

He bent to meet me for the kiss I was after. The moment his lips touched mine he grabbed my ass and pulled me closer. Another rash decision that was going to have him tangled up in my life. As I parted my lips and let his tongue enter my mouth, I knew I wouldn't mind it for the next hour or so. I moaned at the thought. I wove my fingers in his hair and pressed closer.

His erection was an evident rod between us. His lips moved, soft yet firm. He suckled my tongue, a gentle motion I didn't know I'd enjoy until that very moment. I needed friction, something, anything to help get me over the edge. He pressed his thigh between my legs as if reading my mind. I shamelessly humped against him in desperate need.

Emilio broke from the kiss and trailed his nose along my jaw. His warm breath came out in quick bursts as he held fast to my ass, aiding in my movements. He caught the lobe of my ear between his teeth, nipping at it softly before letting it go. "You need it, don'tcha, Ma? Been thirsting over my dick."

He gave my ass a smack like last time and I groaned at the deliciousness. My breath was short and raspy. My nipples scraped against the thin fabric of their confines creating more stimulation. My pussy throbbed against the pressure of Emilio's thigh as I gyrated, getting closer and closer to my release. He snaked one of his hands under my shirt and pulled the cup of my bra down.

I gasped when he pinched my nipple. My body was on fire. My pulse raced and all I wanted, all I could focus on was the "fix" as he'd called it. I gripped his shoulders and rested my head on his chest.

"You been over here touching yourself thinking of me. Bet you had your fingers deep in your wet, wet pussy calling out my name as you made yourself come. Who's making you feel this good? Say it for me."

"Em...Emilio. Fuck!" I screamed as his dirty truths unleashed the orgasm I'd been chasing.

12

EMILIO

I PROPPED MY HANDS UP BEHIND MY HEAD AND RESETTLED ON THE pillow. After she'd recovered, we'd moved the party upstairs, much to the displeasure of Ren who whined and scratched at the door for a while before giving up.

"You hungry?"

She looked over and frowned at me. "Oh, I'm expected to cook for you now?"

I couldn't stop the smile from forming over the attitude in her voice.

"I clearly didn't do a good enough job if you're still so tightly wound." I propped up on one hand and placed my other on her hip and pulled her closer. "Something I'll work on...after I eat."

"Fine. I might have something I can whip up." The coy smile on her lips was in direct contradiction with the annoyance she tried to show.

"Nah, chill out. I got this."

She scooted into a sitting position and unfortunately tucked the sheet around her blocking her tits from view. "You can cook?"

I ran my hands through my hair, moving the stray curls

from my face. "You know, I don't think I've met anyone that could offend me with their skepticism as much as you do. It's a skill you have. Is it just me, or do you think all men are incapable of caring for their basic needs?"

Ma tapped a finger to her chin and looked thoughtful. "It might be just you. And I'm sorry. I shouldn't assume..."

"Yeah, you shouldn't. With all the familial women in my life, I've been yelled at plenty of times to 'get my scrawny butt in here and learn something.' None of them were about to let me sit around thinking I was going to be catered to being the only male besides my pops. From pernil to country fried steak, I got you covered. And, I'm willing to bet I have a better stocked kitchen than you do."

She drew her brows together and downturned her lips. "Now you're pushing it."

"Wanna put a friendly wager on it?" I smiled big at the possibilities of what I'd want my prize to be.

She put her hand out toward me. "You're on."

I grabbed it and gave it a firm shake.

"When I win, you're going to look mighty manly in a bright pink tank top with a sequined Chihuahua on it while you proudly take Yoda on a walk around the complex."

Her eyes were wide and sparkled with amusement. She seemed to be extremely proud of what she thought was an embarrassing win, but I grew up with sisters. That was nothing compared to what they'd put me through.

I rubbed my hands together. "A'ight. I can go with that, but I'm not worried. I'm gonna win this. And when I do, you'll have to go out with me." She started to speak, but I cut her off. "And...for each snarky remark that you make, it adds an extra date." I thought for a minute. "Better yet..."

"Better yet what?"

"Nope, that's for me to know and you to find out after I win."

"I call foul. How can I enter into an agreement if I don't know all the terms?"

I shrugged. "Too late, Ma. We already shook on it. Now, as much as I hate to say it, get your sexy ass dressed. I have a bet to win."

"In your dreams. In fact, if we're adding secret additions, I just came up with one of my own." She gave me a smug look as she twisted her hair into a messy bun. When we got downstairs, Ren looked up, sniffed the air, then proceeded to move so he turned his back to us. Lana just shook her head and headed into the kitchen.

Winning this bet was going to be the perfect cover for getting her on a date. Being fuck buddies was great and all, but I wanted to get to know her more with our clothes on. And with the way she ran hot and cold with me, she probably would have shut me down if I'd asked directly.

This could be a risky move if things turned sour. She wasn't the friendliest before and if she went all "woman scorned" after we split ways there could be hell to pay. However, I already knew I was more than willing to take that chance. I liked her, thorns and all. Ma kept me on my toes. And I was ready to ride this out for as long as it lasted.

"How are we determining? How much we have? How healthy the options are? Or a combo of both?" She leaned against her counter, crossed her arms and waited for an answer.

"We'll go with both," I replied walking over to her fridge. Soon as I opened it I started laughing. "You've already lost."

She stormed over and knocked me out of the way with her hip. "What in the hell are you talking about? I have plenty of food in there for one person. Shopping weekly I get what I need based on my meal plans and I have less waste." She slammed the door shut and glared at me.

"So, you're eating a bell pepper, a package of kale, and drinking almond milk all week?"

Her frown deepened. "You know damned well I had more than that. Plus my meats and stuff are in the freezer you haven't even checked."

I shrugged and smiled. She was so easily annoyed, it was hard not to push those hair-trigger buttons to get her riled up. "Maybe, but I still got this on lock. Anyway, let's go. I have steaks marinating."

She crossed her arms and cocked her head to the side. "Steaks. As in more than one. Mighty presumptuous to assume I'd have dinner with you."

I licked my lips and stepped closer to her. "I like to eat, Ma." I dropped my gaze to her crotch. When I looked back up, her face had turned slightly pink. "But, being the gentleman I am, I'm more than willing to share my...meat with you."

She swallowed and closed her eyes for a brief second. When she lifted her gaze back to meet mine, a slight grin pulled at her lips. "Just...meat isn't a full...dinner."

"Aww, Ma. You know me better than that. You get nothing less than three courses, and if you're good, a midnight snack, too," I added with a wink.

I didn't miss the slight shiver she did. "I...um, need to feed Yoda first."

"Bring him."

The small beast wasn't all bad. Unlike his high-strung owner, he was pretty chill. And like his namesake, he was working some sort of Jedi mind tricks on me, since I was normally a big dog fan, but actually kinda liked the tiny dude. Though it remained way more fun to give her shit than admit that out loud.

Back at my place, Ma got Ren situated. His little ass was not shy about making himself at home on my sofa. I was thankful she brought along a blanket for him so he didn't scratch the leather too much. I walked out to get my grill heated and when

I entered again Ma was standing in the kitchen, fridge open and mouth agape.

"There is no way you eat all of this before it goes bad."

I knew she was looking at the vast assortment of fruits and vegetables I kept stocked. "Check the cabinet bottom left of the fridge."

"A juicer. You have a juicer. Who the hell actually uses one of those?"

"Someone who just won the bet."

What was in there was just the start. She hadn't even seen the lean, butcher cut meats in the freezer. Or the assortment of fresh herbs.

"Fuck me," she muttered.

"Greedy aren't you. But later. We need to refuel first."

She crossed her arms and frowned at me. "You do realize when I say that, I'm not actually requesting that you fuck me, right?"

I placed my hand on my chest in mock surprise. "What? I was certain it was a request. One I'm more than happy to fill. Being a good neighbor and all trying to help another in need."

She nodded slowly, a smile leisurely replacing the frown. "So, like borrowing a cup of sugar, only I'm borrowing what, a dick?"

I barked out a laugh. "Yeah...something like that."

She shook her head. "This is nuts. You know that right. Like we..." She gestured pointing back and forth between us to emphasize her point. "Don't make sense. Outside of admittedly crazy high sexual chemistry, what do we have?"

Whatever we had was new, and fun, and label-less. And that was okay. I wasn't thinking long term, but getting to know my uptight neighbor better was high on my priority list. The playful look on her face had been replaced with the pinched, pissed off look I knew all too well.

I stepped closer, placing my hands on her hips. "Fun, Ma.

We have fun. Why can't we start there and not overthink the rest?"

She looked up at me, frown deepening. "Overthinking is what I do. It's my happy place and it keeps me out of trouble."

I grinned as a thought popped into my head. "Have you been doodling our names together inside hearts on your notebooks?"

She shoved me. "Ew, hell no. And this is the issue. You don't take anything seriously. Everything is a fucking joke to you."

"Whoa, whoa. Slow the fuck down. We can't all have sticks up our asses. There is nothing wrong with having a little fun. No need to spreadsheet everything to death."

"I don't have a stick up my ass."

"You could've fooled me. You clearly turned your bitchy switch on out of no fucking where."

She sucked in a sharp breath. My statement might have been a bit harsh, but damn I hadn't been lying when I said she had a skill for finding new ways to offend me. I may have enjoyed pushing her buttons, but she could get under my skin just as damn easily it seemed.

The woman loved to toss up roadblocks for no damn reason. I seriously didn't even know what the fuck we were fighting about. One minute we were joking about borrowing dick like it was sugar and the next she was acting like...like hell I didn't even know how to explain the foolishness that was unfolding.

Ma opened her mouth to speak but closed it again. Without a word she went to retrieve her dog and walked out of my place. I could have stopped her, and probably should have to figure out what the hell was her issue, but I let her go. Cooling down and regrouping would do us both some good.

13

LANA

What the hell had I just done? My heart raced and my stomach twisted in knots. I held Yoda close, too close as he squirmed and I set him free. Down the hall he ran, far away from my affections. A sad representation of how I always managed to screw something up. I shook my hands and walked in circles in my foyer. I had just acted like some clingy teenager all but demanding he label himself as my boyfriend or some shit.

That wasn't me.

Deep breath in. Slow breath out. It wasn't that serious. But his brush off annoyed me more than it should. Having fun. I could have fun with no strings attached. Only I'd just acted the exact opposite of that.

"Ugh!" I slumped against the wall and slid down to the floor.

Who was I kidding? I wanted all the strings, but it was my inability to properly communicate that sent my past dalliances running for the heels after a while. The whole "not you but me, but really it's you" thing I'd dealt with plenty. I should be used to it by now. My "uptightness" and needing things always done my way didn't bode well for the long term with most men.

Emilio had some magical way of making me let loose and just go with the flow. Sometimes.

The light tap, tap, tap of Yoda's paws echoed down the hall. Moments later he was jumping up on my arm, nosing at my face. I flattened my legs and picked him up. "You get me, bud. You're all the companionship I need."

Yoda curled up in my lap and I absentmindedly stroked his soft fur as I mentally planned out ways to go back to not seeing Emilio in passing. A few minutes later, Yoda's ears perked up and he took off toward the glass slider, barking as he ran. He scratched at the door requesting out but I ignored him. I had no doubt Mr. Frustration was out on his patio and I was not in the mood to deal with any of that. Instead, I headed upstairs away from my dog's whimpering to shower and clear my head.

Clean, but in no better a mood, I grabbed a glass from the cabinet and a bottle of wine from the refrigerator. I poured myself a generous amount before heading toward my living room. Work would be the distraction I needed. Numbers weren't complicated. Numbers didn't have strange, irrational, and way out of place emotions that made you say dumb shit.

I stopped in my tracks at the sight of my annoyance standing on my patio, smile on his face, and a plate in his hand. Part of me thought about closing the blinds in his face, but that would be rude. Ruder than I had already been. With a low sigh, I headed over to open the door.

"I offered you dinner, and I'm one to keep my word," he stated holding the plate out toward me. The medium-rare steak was cut on the plane and spread across a bed of greens topped with some sort of sauce. It was accompanied by mashed potatoes and grilled squash. Damn the man could cook.

I stared at him and sighed. "God, how you annoy me."

He laughed. "What can I say, it seems to be my superpower."

I took the offered food and stepped to the side to let him in. "Where's Ren?"

"Upstairs sleeping in the middle of my bed. Would you like a glass?" I held up my beverage.

"You trying to get me drunk to take advantage?"

"Are you that much of a lightweight that one small glass of wine would knock you out?"

"No, but if it means you'll do some wicked things to me, I can pretend." His dimples deepened when his devilish grin took up residence.

Was he deliberately not bringing up what happened or waiting for me to do it? I knew I probably needed to apologize. Again. But he certainly didn't seem to be bothered in the least. I handed him my wine and pointed to the couch. I joined him a few minutes later with another glass and utensils.

"Thank you for dinner."

He sat back and sipped on the Cabernet. "You're welcome. Enjoy."

"Where's yours?"

He patted his stomach in reply. Ah, so not sharing a meal with me so much as not letting it go to waste. I pushed away the weird feeling of disappointment and stuffed my mouth with the juicy steak to keep myself from saying anything out of place. As I moaned my appreciation, Emilio slid a folded sheet of paper next to my glass.

I glanced at it then over at him. "What's that?"

"Language you understand."

I frowned and put down my fork and knife to pick up the paper. I started coughing when I read the title in large bold print across the top: Reasons Emilio is awesome. Beneath it was a color-coded bar graph. I took a gulp of wine hoping to dislodge the lump that had formed there as I read over the columns.

"You're unbelievable," I managed through lingering coughs.

"Just trying to relate to you on your level." He set his glass down and pulled the paper from my hand. "You're the pro, con type so I figured I'd help you out."

The first category was sex which was a bright bar that he'd taken the time to extend past the confines of the graph so it extended to the top of the paper. Point made. And I couldn't deny it, the sex was off the charts. Literally now. I giggled at the thought.

"I'm not seeing any cons on your handy graph." I looked up at him and his eyes sparkled with amusement.

"Because there aren't any. Even my annoying you is a positive."

"How do you figure that?"

"Easy, because you enjoy it. Yes, I push your buttons from time to time, but never to a point where you don't also push back. Believe me, I have no doubt should I really, truly, piss you off, you'd let me know with a quickness."

I looked away and stabbed the squash and ate it to buy some time. He did annoy me. We had jack shit in common. And he was so not like any other man I'd ever been interested in. My total and complete opposite in all his frustrating glory. Yet, I was drawn to him for some unknown reason. And he seemed to be just as drawn to me.

"We have fun," I whispered mostly to myself.

"We have fun," he agreed.

I looked over at him. "Why am I always the one apologizing?"

"Cuz I'm flawless perfection and never do wrong?" he replied without missing a beat.

I doubled over laughing. Cocky bastard. I wiped tears from

my eyes and got myself under control. "I...I don't think that's it at all, but I'll let you pretend." I took a breath and picked up my wine. "I'm sorry for my behavior earlier," I mumbled from behind my glass.

"It's all good. No harm done."

"No, it's...I don't know why I got all worked up. You do have a talent for making me act out of character. Have since before I even met you."

"Is that a bad thing?"

I took another sip. "Yes. I'm on unfamiliar ground and it makes me uneasy. And no, because I'm learning that being spontaneous isn't all bad."

He slid his hand along the back of my neck and pulled me closer to him. My gaze focused on his lips and I pressed my own together.

"Look, Ma, I know you said overthinking is your happy place and shit, but slow that brain of yours down. I like you. You reluctantly like me."

I laughed at the qualifier he threw in.

"The worst that can happen is we don't work out and you can go back to pretending I don't exist. Until then, if you're willing, let's just enjoy the moment and see where it leads us."

Damn him for making logical and surprisingly well thought out sense.

"Do more dinners come with this deal?"

His pearly whites went on full display. "I thought food was the way to a man's heart."

"I think that is more of a sexist saying to get women to do the cooking."

He nodded and laughed. "If I can get cookies, you can get steak."

I sat back and extended my hand. "Deal."

He grabbed it and shook. "See Ma, who would have

thought you being cordial to me would have worked out so well for both of us."

I leaned forward and kissed him. "Are you going to gloat?"

"Damn right I will."

I smiled and whispered, "Fuck me."

"Yes, ma'am."

EPILOGUE

Six months later

MA SET the steaming mug of black coffee next to my work station and kissed my cheek.

"Morning, sexy. And thanks," I said, giving a quick swat to her ass as she walked away.

"You're welcome. How long have you been up?"

I glanced at the clock in the corner of my PC. "Only about half an hour. I wanted to get a jump on building this tower. Well, rebuilding best I can after their botched attempt. Seriously who the fuck orders computer parts instead of just one already built if they've never done it before? Folks think they can learn everything from watching damn YouTube or some shit."

I pushed my glasses up to the crown of my head and watched the hypnotic sway of her hips as she went to join Ren on the futon. The T-shirt she wore barely covered her and her panty-less bottom peeked out as a tease beneath the white cotton.

"Beats me. I wouldn't even know what to order." She spoke through a yawn.

"That's what you have me for."

She folded her shapely legs under her and nodded. "Yup, just one of the many reasons I keep you around." She blew an air kiss in my direction.

"Glad to know I've not outlived my usefulness."

In the months we'd been dating our differences had worked to our advantage. She'd slowly taken over the billing aspect of my business, suggesting better accounting software and keeping way more detailed records than I'd cared to. She was the spreadsheet and numbers wizard so I let her have at it. I knew she needed the semblance of order, and I honestly didn't mind conceding to her on some things.

Meanwhile anytime someone at her company had computer issues she sent them to me, and I'd somehow become their unofficial after-hours IT person.

The spending nights together had evolved like everything else, on its own without much thought—on my part—being given or what it meant being dissected. Most of those nights were at my place and I'd made plenty of jokes about her using me to get the unit she was originally after. Not that I minded if it meant her being the last person I saw at night and the first one in the mornings.

I slid my glasses back in place and returned my attention to the tower in front of me. My gaze went to the drawer to my right. I licked my lips and picked up the mug. Hopefully the bitter liquid would help replace the moisture that had drained from my mouth. Where the fuck had nerves come from? This was nuts. Her damned overthinking habit had rubbed off on me at the worst damn time.

I'd already made up my mind. Yet, I'd been sitting on that decision for well over a week, thinking through all the possible roadblocks she could throw my way. But I knew this was the right move. I shot a look over to where she sat sipping her tea and flipping through the papers she'd left on the table the night before.

I'd put a desk in the third bedroom so she'd have a place to work, but most times she ended up right where she was, curled up on the futon while we each worked without disturbing each other. I pulled open the drawer and grabbed the gold box that had been hidden in there for the last week.

"Heads up," I called out. She looked up and I tossed it to her.

"Oh shit. What the hell?"

Ren lifted his head and if I didn't know better, I'd swear his little ass scowled at us before he jumped down and left the room. I was sure he was headed to the guest bedroom since he'd quickly claimed that space as his own. Sleeping most nights in the middle of the queen-sized bed.

"Got you something."

"I can see that, but could you give it to me like a normal person?"

"Where's the fun in that?"

Thank fuck my voice didn't betray the full-fledged nerves that took over at that moment. I watched in silence as she lifted the gold cardboard lid to reveal the blue velvet box contained within.

Lana looked up at me. "Emilio?"

I took my glasses off and set them next to the coffee mug. "Are you going to open it?"

Keeping her eyes on me, she dumped the smaller box into the palm of her hand. It opened with a soft creak and she finally tore her gaze away to look down. She didn't say a word, which did jack shit for my peace of mind. In slow motion, she put the box down and walked over to me. Leaning down, she kissed me. Our lips connected, soft at first, but the intensity quickly took over. Tongues mashed together and I stood, keeping our connection. I grabbed at her bare ass pulling her close. She broke free and yanked me from my office toward our bedroom. *Our.* Yeah, I liked the sound of that.

With a quick shove, Ma pushed me back so I fell onto the bed. I didn't even get to speak as she made quick work of discarding her T-shirt. My dick tented my boxers but not for long as she pulled them free before straddling me. Again our mouths met. I palmed her tits, squeezing them and letting my thumbs graze across her hard nipples. Fuck, I didn't care she hadn't answered me, the only thing that mattered was the warmth of her body that surrounded me as she lowered herself.

I'd never get tired of the skin to skin feel of being inside her sans condom. A trip to the doctor for STI screening and the fact she had an IUD made this glorious moment possible. She looked at me, eyes wide and glassy and began to move. Slow and easy. I grabbed her ass and lifted my head to capture one of her nipples in my mouth as her breasts swung forward.

She pushed herself up, palms flat against my stomach. I groaned when she clenched around me. An amazing trick of fucking me damn near without moving. She sucked me in and held me tight and goddamn it felt wondrous, but what I wanted was something more. I smacked her ass.

"Come on, sexy. None of this tentative shit. Fuck me like you mean it."

She let out a little gasp and fell forward. She pumped her hips up and down, fast and furious. Nails dug into my shoulders and I kept a tight grip on her ass meeting her thrust for thrust. Hot breaths and soft grunts filled the room.

I loved this position. Being able to watch as she rode me hard. Seeing each change in expressions on her face. The biting of her lips, the closing of her eyes. And best of all, the movement of her tits. I loved watching them sway and sucking on her nipples while she fucked me like I owed her money.

Her pussy clenched and her body shuddered with her release. My own followed not long after. Neither of us moved and she rested her head on my shoulder. The longer the silence stretched on the more I worried the sex was a distraction.

She looked up at me, a slight smile tugging at her lips. "You realize that was the world's crappiest proposal, right?"

"Was this a yes?"

She nodded.

The boulder of doubt that had been sitting on my chest broke apart. I grabbed her ass and gave it a squeeze. "Well, it got me laid and a fiancée, so I'd say it was a damned good one."

———

THANK YOU

Thank you for purchasing Being Cordial. I hope you enjoyed the story. If you are so inclined, I'd appreciate a review. If you enjoyed this story, be sure to catch up with the other residents of Desert Rose Station in *Being Neighborly* and *Being Hospitable*!

Until next time,
Meka

ABOUT THE AUTHOR

Meka James is a writer of adult contemporary and erotic romance. A born and raised Georgia Peach, she still resides in the southern state with her hubby of 16 years and counting. Mom to four kids of the two legged variety, she also has four fur-babies of the canine variety. Leo the turtle and Spade the snake rounds out her wacky household. When not writing or reading, Meka can be found playing The Sims 3, sometimes Sims 4, and making up fun stories to go with the pixelated people whose world she controls.

You can sign up for my newsletter at:
www.authormekajames.com

OTHER BOOKS BY MEKA

Being Neighborly

*Book 1 of the Desert Rose Hook-ups

Being Hospitable

*Book 2 of the Desert Rose Hook-ups

Fiendish: A Twisted Fairytale

please note this book tackles dark themes that may be upsetting to readers. You don't have to read Fiendish to read and enjoy Not Broken

Not Broken: The Happily Ever After

*Continuation of Calida's story from Fiendish

The Lists

*Extended HEA for Calida and Malcolm from Not Broken

Anything Once

*Erotic romance featuring Ian and Quinn Faraday who are on a journey to spice up their sex lives

CONNECT WITH ME!

Social media
To connect with me, please follow me at the following sites:
Meka's Musings
Twitter
Instagram
Tumblr
Facebook

Get up-to-date news by signing up for my newsletter
MEKA'S MUSINGS

Made in the USA
Las Vegas, NV
04 February 2025